The Story Setting

TABLE OF CONTENTS

You Can't Catch ME!

BROCK TURNER

Illustrated by Brenda Cantell

sundance

A Haights Cross Communications ✈ Company

The Story Characters

Jenny

Steve

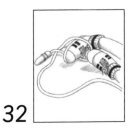

CHAPTER 1

Jenny Can't Run

At lunchtime everyone played tag.

Jenny was always one of the first to get caught.

Steve made fun of Jenny. He said that she was a slow runner. He said that she had snail legs. He said that she would never catch him.

After you got caught, you had to chase the other kids. Jenny spent lots of time chasing the others.

Steve Is a Show-Off

Steve was a pretty fast runner. He was always one of the last kids to get caught. He was also a show-off, a big loudmouthed show-off.

"You can't catch me! You can't catch me!" chanted Steve. He stood just out of Jenny's reach.

Boy! Oh boy! This made Jenny angry.
She ran after him. But he moved out
of her way.

Steve stopped right in front of Jenny again.

Some of the kids should have helped Jenny catch Steve. Instead, they stood and watched.

Jenny was fed up. She'd had enough.
Jenny wanted to beat Steve at
something.

Just then, she said to Steve, "I bet I can jump rope longer than you can."

"No way," said Steve. "We're playing tag, not jump rope! And you can't catch me."

CHAPTER  3

Chicken

A few of the kids giggled. Jenny didn't like it. She felt like running away.

Jenny felt shy, and her face turned red. But then she saw the grin on Steve's face. He knew he'd won again.

Jenny couldn't let them laugh at her.
She looked at Steve and said, "I think
you're chicken."

Then she made a noise like a chicken.
"Brrrkkk! Brrrkkk! Brrrkkk!" Now the
other kids were laughing at Steve.

Jenny could see that he didn't like being laughed at.

Good. Now Steve knows how it feels, she thought.

"I'm not chicken," said Steve. Then he turned to walk away.

Jenny made the chicken noises again.

"Brrrkkk! Brrrkkk! Brrrkkk! You're a scaredy-cat!" she yelled.

Everyone laughed. A few of the kids
started making chicken noises, too.

"OK, OK," said Steve, "I'll jump rope. But we start at the same time. And the first one to stop loses."

"Sounds fair to me," said Jenny. She was a little scared. She really wanted to beat Steve.

CHAPTER 4

Jumping Rope

Jenny got her jump rope out of her bag. Steve borrowed one.

Now the playground was packed with kids. Everyone wanted to see who would win.

Jenny hated that everyone was staring at her. Steve even looked a little nervous, too.

Sally told them to get ready. She counted down, "3, 2, 1, GO!"

Jenny and Steve started to jump. By now, most of the school was watching them.

The Winner!

The two kids jumped rope for a few minutes. Then Jenny began to get tired.

Jenny tried to jump slower.

Slower will be easier, she thought.

Then Jenny caught her foot in the rope. She almost tripped. But then she started to think that Steve would beat her. Again!

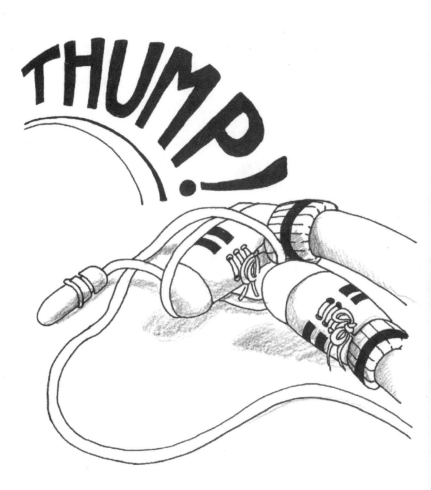

Suddenly, there was a thump beside
her. Steve had tripped. She had won!

Jenny thought that she would feel
great, but she didn't. She was upset.

She looked down at Steve sitting on the ground. He had a bloody knee. The other kids were laughing at him.

"Are you all right, Steve?" Jenny
asked.

"Of course I'm OK," Steve grunted.

"Look," said Jenny, "you're good at tag, and I'm good at jump rope."

"So what?" said Steve.

"Soooo . . ." said Jenny, "you're not better than me, and I'm not better than you. No more teasing. OK?"

Steve didn't say anything for a minute. Then he muttered, "OK."

The school bell rang. It was time to line up to go back into class.

After school, Jenny ran outside to meet her mom.

"See you tomorrow, Steve," she called.

"Yeah," he shouted and waved. "Bye."

Making a friend is better than winning, Jenny thought.

GLOSSARY

chanted
repeated in a
sing-song way

grunted
made a deep, short
sound like a pig

loudmouthed
acting bratty and
speaking too loudly

nervous
timid, scared

scaredy-cat
a coward

shy
very timid

tripped
stumbled

Brock Turner

Brock's favorite thing to do is eat a big lunch and then lie around in the sun daydreaming. Brock thinks that having an imagination is the most important thing—even better than having a computer game. An imagination can make you laugh, get you out of trouble, even make you rich! When Brock is rich and famous, he will have chocolate cake for dinner every night. Imagine that!

Brenda Cantell

Brenda used to be a television art director. Now she's an illustrator, which she likes because she can design her own sets and costumes, choose her own props, and cast her own actors. She lives by a river with her husband, Ben, and a lizard who lives in the roof.

Published by Sundance Publishing
P.O. Box 1326, 234 Taylor Street, Littleton, MA 01460
800-343-8204

Copyright © text Brock Turner
Copyright © illustrations Brenda Cantell

First published 1999 as Sparklers by
Blake Education, Locked Bag 2022, Glebe 2037, Australia
Exclusive United States Distribution: Sundance Publishing

ISBN 0-7608-8005-0

Printed in Canada